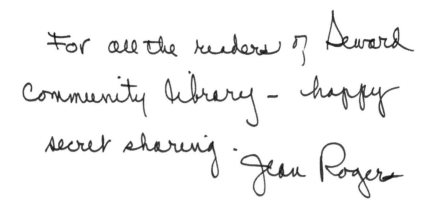

For all the readers of Seward Community Library — happy secret sharing. — Jean Rogers

JEAN ROGERS

The Secret Moose

illustrated by Jim Fowler

GREENWILLOW BOOKS NEW YORK

Printed in the United States of America
First Edition   1 2 3 4 5 6 7 8 9 10

Library of Congress Cataloging in Publication Data

Rogers, Jean.
The secret moose.
Summary: A young boy living in Alaska
develops an interest in moose and their
habits after he sees a moose in his
backyard and decides to follow it.
1. Moose—Juvenile fiction.
2. Children's stories, American.
[1. Moose—Fiction. 2. Alaska—Fiction.]
I. Fowler, Jim, ill.   II. Title.
PZ10.3.R63Se 1985   [Fic]   84-12897
ISBN 0-688-04248-1
ISBN 0-688-04249-X (lib. bdg.)

For all the S's and G's who have enriched
my life for the past thirty-six years

CHAPTER ONE

Gerald was the only one to see the moose. Anita, who was usually the one who saw (and did) everything first, was too busy telling her mother for the four thousand, nine hundred and sixty-sixth time just how much she hated oatmeal. Dad was hidden behind his newspaper.

"Y-y-yuck," Anita was saying loudly.

Gerald barely heard her, he was so intent

on the moose. It was having breakfast too. It was pulling and munching at the willow branches along the stream that bordered the Perrys' backyard. Their barn stood next to the stream, at the far end of the yard. A corral for Charcoal, Anita's black pony, faced south so that it could catch the most of the winter sun, and it was bounded on one side by the water.

It was the first week of May, but snow and

slushy ice still clung to the stream's shores. The willows were in bud, but the road in front of the house was a sea of mud and the snow piled up along the road was hidden beneath a coating of dirt and gravel. Charcoal's corral was bare and squelchy with mud. It was spring in Gold Stream Valley.

"You've still your pony to tend," Mother warned Anita.

Gerald shoveled in his own oatmeal auto-matically, uncomplaining, and watched the moose move deeper into the willows which grew thickly on both sides of the stream. It was harder to see the moose now. Gerald opened his mouth to tell Dad and Mom and Anita to look quickly before it was gone. Then he shut his mouth. Suddenly he realized he didn't want anyone else to see the moose.

"Well, I'm off," Dad said. He left in his usual flurry of kisses and snatched-up lunch. Anita got up too, to put on her parka and boots and take Charcoal some fresh water and hay. Gerald ate another piece of toast as he watched her blue-jacketed figure hurry across the yard to the barn. He had a special feeling of satisfaction, part toast and jam satis-faction and part satisfaction that he'd kept the moose a secret from Anita. He went to get his own parka.

"Here, take Anita's lunch out to the bus with you, and remind her that it's my late night at the library," said his mother. "And I'd like her to start dinner."

After school, as soon as the bus brought them home, Anita went straight to the barn and Charcoal. Gerald went around the house to the rear door. Leaving his boots in the entry, he padded into the kitchen in search of food. Balancing a glass of milk and a handful of gingersnaps, he managed to step back into his muddy boots and get out the door again.

Anita took Charcoal out to the road for a ride in the only possible space this time of year. She paid no attention to Gerald sitting on the step as she rode by. As soon as she was safely out of the drive, he headed for the wil-

lows where he had seen the moose that morning. He found its tracks easily. The moose had obviously come from down-stream, working its way up browsing. He knelt down beside the tracks. Getting up, he followed them to the water's edge, about where he had watched the moose disappear into the brush. It would be miles away now, probably. He hoped so. Unwelcome thoughts of men with dogs and guns came to his mind. The hunting season wasn't until fall, but here in Gold Stream Valley there were people who hunted out of season.

Still following the hoof marks in the snow, Gerald stepped onto the slushy ice. By the Perrys' yard the stream was wide and shallow with sandy islands that for a brief period during the peak of break-up were covered totally. Only the largest had enough high ground to stay above water. The tracks led to one of these islands. During the summer Gerald and Lexie had fixed up a camp on it before the mosquitoes' arrival had made it unbearable.

Gerald lost the moose's tracks but decided to have a look at the camp before searching for them again. The willows were so dense, it was hard to make his way through the forest of twigs and whippy branches. Then he saw the moose lying in a snowbank. It's dead! he thought. He stood perfectly still, shocked at stumbling on it. The creature looked enormous, a mountain of gray-brown. Gerald noticed the black hooves, the nostrils shining wetly, the hairs swirling around the nose.

Then the moose opened an eye. It was alive. Fear swept over Gerald. He'd been warned and warned that wild animals when surprised were particularly dangerous. But the moose was also afraid. Gerald could see its muscles bunch with the effort to get to its feet. After a brief struggle it sank back. Then Gerald, his own muscles gathering to run, saw the wound. It was covered with dried blood, a trickle oozing bright red through the darker edges. Was the moose dying?

"Oh, you poor thing," Gerald said softly. The moose made another attempt to rise. Gerald backed away a bit, still speaking softly. "Oh, that looks awful. What happened to you?" The sight of that ugly gash on the moose's flank made him feel sick. He couldn't bear to think of the hurt. When he had watched the moose feeding that morning, he hadn't noticed anything wrong.

Gerald squatted down and watched. When had it happened? The moose closed the eye he could see. Was it dead now or just sleeping? As he crouched there, he became gradually aware of the soft sounds all around him: the slight noise of the water, a dog barking in the distance, birds twittering. He thought, straining to hear and holding his own breath carefully, that he could hear the moose breathing. Now he could see the slight in-and-out of the animal's breath. The relief he felt filled him completely. He watched the sleeping moose until a cramp in his leg forced him to stand up. The moose's eye opened, gave him a quick look, and closed again. This time the moose made no effort to stand up. He decided it was a good sign.

Finally Gerald crept away. He backed cautiously at first, then turned and moved as quietly as he could across the slushy stream. When he came onto the shore, he stepped carefully in all the moose tracks he could find and smoothed them out. He didn't think why, he just continued to wipe out the moose's tracks as he made his way home.

Kicking off his boots, he went to the telephone and dialed his mother's work number. "Hi, Mom. Nothing's wrong, don't worry. I just want you to bring me a book. I want something that tells me all about a moose."

"I think the Fairbanks Public Library can manage that. Is Anita there?"

"She's out on Charcoal."

"I don't suppose Dad is home yet?"

"No, not yet. Oh, Mom, bring me one I can read. Don't forget."

"I won't forget. 'Bye, hon."

CHAPTER TWO

That evening right after dinner, Gerald took the two books his mother had brought him to his room. In the front of the first book was a big green map of Alaska showing the areas where moose could usually be found. For a long time Gerald looked at it. His own home, Fairbanks, was a little red dot near the center of the state.

The book told about a bear trying to attack a moose calf and how the mother moose had defended the calf and driven the bear away. Looking at the pictures, Gerald realized his moose was a female, a cow. She had no calf, but neither did she have antlers, and she fit perfectly the book's description of looking more like a horse than a deer. Again a sense of awe filled Gerald as he thought of the moose lying there, so huge, so still, with that great, bloody gash on her rear hindquarter.

Gerald plodded on through the book. His reading was not up to some of the larger words, but there were pictures on every page. He read that when a moose was happy, it flicked its ears, and when it was fearful, the ears stood up straight and alert. When angry, a moose laid back its ears, the hairs of its mane stood up, and it gave warning grunts.

Gerald thought all this information might come in handy so he read it over twice. If his moose gave any warning signals, ears or otherwise, he wanted to understand in a hurry.

In bed that night, Gerald lay awake for a while sorting out the facts he had been reading. He thought about the moose lying in the willow thicket. Would it still be there tomorrow?

Next day Gerald fidgeted at school until Mrs. Means scolded him for not paying attention. He dashed out so fast he forgot his lunch pail and had to go back for it. The bus had never seemed so pokey. Would the moose be gone? Of course she will be gone, he told himself. She was just resting her bad leg until she could go on. He knew that no wild creature would stay in an area so close to civilization.

But when Gerald crossed the stream and made his way carefully to the island, the moose was still there. She was lying exactly as he had left her yesterday, and again he thought she might be dead. As he came closer, she lifted her head and gave him a brief glance, then sank back as if too tired to do more. She kept her eye open though. For a long time Gerald crouched quietly at her side and watched. Her hind leg was stretched out stiffly, the wound looked as grisly as ever. The edges of the cut were black and rough, but the center still glistened bright red.

Gerald could see where the moose had been feeding. At least she wasn't starving. The willow branches within reach were broken and the bark stripped away, just as a picture in the book had shown. Probably, he thought, if the moose was able to eat, it meant she wasn't going to die. He watched her huge belly move gently with her breathing. Her jaws were moving slightly too, in a faint chewing motion. Of course, she was chewing a cud. That's what the book said moose did while they rested.

The scent of the willow buds was strong and pleasing. No wonder the moose liked to

eat them. The wet earth smelled good too: dank, strong, and leafy. He squatted for a long time, enjoying the smells and the sounds before he got up. As he backed carefully away, the moose raised her head and looked at him. Now he could see both her eyes. Her ears flicked, lazily, and she made no effort to get up. "Goodbye, Moose," Gerald whispered softly. "Stay safe and I'll see you tomorrow."

Gerald had forgotten that it was Wednesday when Anita had her 4-H meeting. On meeting days it was his job to look after Charcoal. He had only remembered it when she wasn't on the bus. He debated giving Charcoal some fresh water and ignoring the rest, but Anita would surely know. Gerald didn't know how she could tell whether or not her pony had been out of the corral, but she could and the fuss she would make wasn't worth the risk. Maybe he could sneak a quick look to see if the moose was still there before he saddled Charcoal, but no, he was supposed to get her out and ride before the homecoming cars made the road dangerous. He must have Charcoal back in the barn by four forty-five to be on the safe side. Sighing, he kicked off his boots and went into the kitchen for a quick snack. He slipped a packet of graham crackers and an apple into his jacket pockets and looked in the sugar cube box. Rats, it was empty, which meant he would have to coax Charcoal with a carrot. Gerald hated catching and bridling the pony. She would come for Anita's whistle, but, though Gerald did not like to admit it, his whistle was puny and thin and Charcoal treated it with contempt.

"Just let her know you mean business,

Gerald," Anita told him over and over. "Don't let her get away with it. As soon as she knows you're the boss, she won't try any more tricks." Anita didn't like to give Charcoal sugar, although she generally kept a box of cubes around for emergencies, the nature of which Gerald didn't know and didn't want to find out. He used them because it was quickest. He didn't mind the riding part, al-

though he didn't have the faith Anita had that Charcoal wouldn't slip and fall with him when the roads were at their iciest.

Today he turned down the road and let Charcoal have her head. The pony, happy to be out, trotted briskly, bouncing Gerald unmercifully. He endured it until Charcoal got the friskiness out of her legs and was content to slow to a walk. When she did, Gerald ate his graham crackers and then his apple, putting the core carefully back in his pocket to

give the pony when they returned. He won-
dered briefly if the moose would enjoy an apple core as much as the pony did. With that
thought he turned Charcoal homeward.
Maybe Anita could tell if the pony had been
out, but even old Eagle Eye couldn't know for
how long. There was still time to check on his
moose.

He was just turning into the drive when his
mother's car came up behind him. He reined
Charcoal near the back step and slid down
while Anita and Mrs. Perry got out.

"Mrs. Berner let us out early today," Anita
said. "How come you're back already?"

"Oh, is it early?" Gerald looked vaguely at
his arm as though to read the time there, although he knew his watch was upstairs in his
bedroom.

"Then you've still got time for a ride," he

added. "Charcoal's not a bit tired." Besides, he thought gleefully, then you will have to put her away.

Anita was already dropping her books and lunch pail and reaching for the bridle.

"Put my stuff in, will you, Gerald?" Anita called back as she and Charcoal headed toward the road. He helped his mother carry groceries in from the car, emptied the garbage and put in a fresh plastic sack, and hastily set the table before he ventured to say he was going out. "I'll just be down by the barn," he said. Mrs. Perry had her head in the refrigerator as he made for the door.

"Okay, just don't go wandering off. Early dinner and I do hope your father remembers. Maybe I'd better call and see if he's left yet." He was safely out the door before she had reached the telephone.

CHAPTER THREE

The moose was still where Gerald had left her, her rear leg sticking out stiffly. It looked as if she hadn't moved at all and Gerald had a bad moment before he realized her eye was open and watching him steadily. Gerald stopped, barely breathing. Slowly the moose raised her head as if to look at him straight on, her ears flicked forward and back, her nose twitched. She shifted her front feet and Gerald readied himself to back off if she rose, but she tucked her legs back under her and laid her head down again. She watched him now with both eyes. Gerald felt sure it was a friendly look.

He stood without moving for what seemed a very long time. The moose watched him, breathing quietly, chewing her cud. Gradually Gerald noticed that the willows within reach had been thoroughly browsed; nothing remained except the thicker branches. He knew from his reading that as big an animal as a moose needed to eat a tremendous amount. Was his moose hungry, starving even? Did it mean she couldn't get up?

While the wound on her leg looked horrible, would it be enough to keep her down if she was really hungry? He thought of the

Shepards' dog; he had only three legs but got around somehow; he could even run. The moose had managed to get to this island. But she might have something else wrong with her, something he couldn't see. He decided to cut some willow tops for her. As always, he backed away carefully, reaching into his pocket for his knife. There was his apple core, saved for Charcoal. Opening his knife, he cut

a long stick of willow and stuck the apple core on the end of it. Now we'll see if moose like apples, he thought. Twice the apple core fell off as he was trying to weave it through the brush to get it close enough for the moose to sniff it. There wasn't enough left of the apple to make it easy to pierce, but on the third try, by inching it along with great patience, Gerald managed to get his tidbit within range. He had to lie flat on his stomach and stretch to his limit, but he did it. The moose ignored the apple core, but when the tip of the willow came within reach, she took it in her mouth unhesitatingly, her great rubbery upper lip pulling it quickly in. The core fell off and the moose paid no attention to it. Gerald wriggled back and began to cut more willow. It was hard work; the willows were green and tough and hard to cut, even at their tender tips. He needed something better than his pocket knife. He made a pile of his few cuttings and started back to the barn when he heard his mother calling him for dinner.

By the time the family had eaten, and his parents had issued orders for the evening, Gerald had made his plans. When they left, he said goodbye absentmindedly. Usually he made a routine protest about Anita being left in charge.

"I'm going down to the barn," Anita said. "Me, too," said Gerald. He gathered up the canvas log carrier from the cupboard by the fireplace and the pruning shears from the barn and went back to the island. Anita was with Charcoal and paid no attention to him.

Gerald spread the log carrier flat on the ground and began cutting willows with the pruning shears. He whacked away happily until he had a good load, though his fingers

ached from maneuvering the shears, and the
tangy, bitter smell of cut willow filled his nose.
He thought if he were a moose it would smell
like supper cooking.

As he approached the moose with his offering, he was faced with a new problem: how to get the twigs within her reach without getting dangerously close. He had heard enough stories of the foolishness of feeding bears or other wild creatures not to take the warnings lightly, even if the moose seemed unable or unwilling to get up.

The moose watched him calmly as he inched his way closer with his awkward load.

It was impossible to move quietly. The log carrier full of willow had to be lifted over the thick undergrowth or pushed through. Gerald was sweating with effort by the time he had gotten himself and his load as near to the moose as he thought safe. He took the longest branch and poked it toward the moose. He was still too far away. He wormed his way a bit closer, lay down flat on his stomach, and pushed the branch a bit farther. He stretched as far as he could, repeating his performance with the apple core. The moose did her part too, stretching her head and grabbing the willow eagerly.

After a few more painstaking tries at pushing single branches forward, Gerald realized he'd be here all night at this rate and Anita would be looking for him soon. She wouldn't give an inch when it came to enforcing his bedtime.

Gerald was tempted to risk just stepping up with his load and dumping it in front of the moose. Surely he could drop it and run faster than this huge, ungainly creature could get up and charge him. But his legs refused to move. He couldn't bring himself to go closer. Sighing, Gerald got slowly to his feet and backed away. He crossed the stream and raced for the barn. He came back carrying the leaf rake.

Again the moose raised her head as he approached. She watched him eagerly and seemed to know he was trying to help. Carefully he piled his collection of willow twigs onto the leaf rake and pushed it cautiously along the ground toward the moose. Lying

flat again, he pushed his load forward, stretching as far as he could. He was losing twigs all along the way, but he managed to turn the rake over and deposit a few within reach of the wounded animal. As fast as he could, he cut another log carrier load and another. He was managing his fourth load when he heard Anita's call. He didn't dare give her an answering shout. Quickly he gathered up a few more willow branches and repeated his performance with the rake. Then seeing how much he had spilled along the path the rake had made, he turned it over and quickly raked up as much as he could. In his haste he wasn't careful enough, the rake caught on a root and the handle banged him on the lip. It was a nasty clip that brought tears to his eyes and a startled cry to his lips. Through a blur he saw the moose perk up her ears, but she never stopped chewing as he backed away, picking up his shears and log carrier on the way. He managed to hang up the tools and get to the house with the log carrier before Anita appeared at the back door to call him again.

"It's about time—"she started. "Whatever did you do to your lip? It's bleeding!"

"I ran into a willow branch," Gerald mumbled. His lip was throbbing, but the pain was worth it. In the bustle of getting him an ice cube to stop the bleeding and deal with the swelling, Anita didn't notice his muddy front and generally disheveled state. She even forgot the usual argument about whose bath night it was.

In bed, still smelling richly of willow, earth, and spring, Gerald tried to figure out how to streamline his feed-the-moose operation, until he fell asleep.

CHAPTER FOUR

For the next four days Gerald felt as if he had never done anything but cut willow branches. He hurried to the island as soon as the school bus deposited him at his door, grabbing his equipment on the way. He had finished the book about moose and what it said was true. These big animals ate and ate and ate to keep up with the demands of their enormous bodies. No matter how hard he worked, the amount of willow he could cut for his moose seemed pitifully small. His mother's call for dinner always came far too soon. The time he could work after dinner was limited, though it was still daylight at this time of year. Both Gerald and Anita had to go to bed long before the sun went down.

Mom said when he came in this evening, "You smell like willow, Gerald. Whatever have you been doing? You're good and filthy, I must say."

"I've been over at Lexie's and my camp." Gerald squirmed away from his mother.

"Well, do you have to get down and just wallow in the dirt?" Good, Gerald thought. Not a serious offense. But he took special pains with his bath that night, using soap liber-

ally and actually scrubbing his hands. Around his fingernails there was a line of green that wouldn't come off. He smelled it critically. Bitter willow.

When his mother came in to kiss him good-night, she admired his clean and shining state. Gerald thought it would be a good time to approach her about the book.

"Can you get me that book to keep?" he asked as his mother was leaving his room.

"Which book are you talking about, hon?"

"The one you brought me about the moose in Alaska. You know, the one I've been reading. It's on my desk."

"You mean you want a copy of your own, Gerald? This one, here. *Deneki*?"

Gerald nodded. "Will it cost much? I could take some money out of the bank. Couldn't I, Mom?"

"Why, Gerald!" Mom stood for a moment with her hand on the light switch. "I'll look in at the bookstore tomorrow, and if they don't have a copy, I'll order one for you. I don't

think it will be necessary to break the bank.''
Mom gave him a smile and turned out the light.

"You won't forget, will you?'' Gerald called softly.

"No, I won't forget. Good night, hon.''

The next afternoon the weather had turned so warm Gerald shed his jacket on the back steps before he headed for the barn and his willow-cutting equipment. He heard Anita talking to Charcoal in the paddock as he walked past, the pruning shears and canvas sling under his arm, rake in hand. He splashed across the water to the island, put down his things, and crept forward. Tiny new leaves were now showing everywhere and the light was a pale greeny gold down here in the thick of the willows. The sun had warmed everything and turned the whole world green—grass tussocks, the opening leaves of the birch trees, the willow, every twig was showing its own special green.

Gerald stood still a moment, taking everything in, watching and smelling.

Then he worked his way quietly forward to check on his moose before he began his harvesting. The air seemed more than usually alive with the sound of birds. Mosquitoes were beginning to make their appearance; this heat would finish the spring hatching in short order.

At first Gerald couldn't believe his eyes. His moose was standing, head lowered, pushing at something in the grass. It took him awhile to make it all out. But when the something began to wriggle, squirm, and separate itself into long skinny legs flailing to find firm ground, he realized it was a moose calf. It must have been just minutes after the birth. If he'd been a little earlier getting home from school, he might even have seen it being born!

The moose cow continued her licking and urging. She was so intent on this that she didn't give Gerald the usual greeting—the calm appraisal and a quiet flick of her ears. Gerald forgot the warnings he had heard about wild mothers and their babies. He simply stood transfixed and watched as the calf responded to its mother's shoves and tried to stand. It looked like a bundle of sticks moving every which way; legs attached so haphazardly it would never get them sorted out, front ones from back ones, and be able to stand. But it did! In a matter of moments it was up, down, up again, and wobbling like a pile of unsteady blocks, reeling around, finally seemingly by accident finding its mother's teat and

the supply of milk. The moose turned her head and watched the calf as it drank. Its little rump twitched; its tiny stub of tail waved and switched.

Finally the moose turned and looked at Gerald. Her ears flipped forward and back, forward and back. Then she turned to look again at the busy calf, then back to Gerald.

As if to say, Gerald thought, see what we did. Aren't you proud? Every muscle tensed, Gerald ached with keeping still. Then he noticed the moose was chewing, and relaxed slightly. If she thought he was any danger to her calf, she wouldn't be calmly chewing her cud.

When the calf stopped suckling, it tried its legs a bit, managing to get all four working in the same direction. More than once, Gerald had to stifle a laugh that rose in his throat. The moose began to browse, reaching up for buds and leaves over her head. Occasionally she tossed a look in Gerald's direction. The calf grew steadier by the minute and began a frisky, almost nimble hop, but never very far from its mother. The cow became more and more engrossed in eating, moving along the stream with a steady breaking of branches, chewing continually, a great machine, cutting and chewing. It was so much more efficient and speedy than Gerald's poor efforts with the shears that it left him gasping. How had she managed with his small offerings?

Gerald eased himself into a comfortable sitting position and watched, entranced. The calf had two more feedings before, suddenly tired, it folded up its long sticks, tucked its nose into a fold of foreleg, gave a trembling, snorty sigh, and closed its eyes. The moose ate a while longer, throwing glances between bites at her sleeping baby, ears flicking, nose flung up every few minutes. Presently she, too, lay down beside her calf. She turned a lazy eye toward Gerald, chewing calmly. The book had said that moose don't have keen eyesight but rely on their sense of smell, and Gerald felt his moose knew him. (All was well now.) The moose's wound was healing too. It had blackened, dried edges, no fresh red anymore. It was getting smaller, closing up.

Gerald watched the moose and her calf until foraging mosquitoes drove him away. At his first movement the moose's ears were up and she opened an eye. Gerald froze. But the eye closed again, her ears relaxed. Gerald gathered up his log carrier, rake, and shears and splashed back across the water, which had melted. His boots glistened clean and black when he crossed Charcoal's yard. Anita had returned from her ride and was, as usual, carrying on a brisk conversation with her pony. Had he been gone that long? It hadn't been more than half an hour at the most. He hung the tools in the barn. He thought he might as well use the log carrier so he put some wood from the shed in it and carried it

up to the house. The fireplace would stand cold until next fall and the log bin was nearly empty. He was folding the canvas carrier when his mother came in.

"Oh, there you are. Just in time to set the table for me. Heavens, are you actually carrying in wood without being asked?" She looked at him suspiciously. "What have you been up to?"

Gerald laughed. "Nothing," he said. "I've been fixing up our camp, but the mosquitoes are getting too bad." He followed his mother out to the kitchen.

"Wash your hands first," she ordered. "By the way, *Deneki* is out of print, but I think I'm going to get you a copy from Margaret. She said her son used to have a copy and if it's still around you can have it. I'll find out tomorrow."

CHAPTER FIVE

All the next day Gerald thought about his moose and her calf and where they might be. He headed slowly for the island as soon as he came home, slowly because he knew he would find them gone. They would have to go up to higher and safer ground, he realized, away from people and dogs and guns. He even wanted them to go, but he couldn't help hoping he'd get one more glimpse to say goodbye.

Even before he approached the spot as quietly as ever, he could tell they were gone. He stood in the center of the island for a long time, listening, separating out the sounds. A dog barking down the valley, a light plane somewhere in the distance, occasional cars going by on the road, birds everywhere, a mosquito's hum right by his ear. He slapped at it. He wandered around the cleared space, eyeing the broken and smashed willows, following the moose's trail. They'd surely go upstream, he thought. That way led farther and farther into wilderness. He wandered along until he finally found another patch of broken and stripped willow branches. Ah, sure enough they had gone upstream. Gerald continued on, half hoping he would catch up with

them, but not really expecting to. Moose could travel miles a day, even foraging with a calf. Besides, if he met his moose away from their own shared island, would she know him or would she charge him like any other intruder? He sat down for a while in the sun and listened, but he knew the moose and her calf were gone.

He was sitting on the back step drinking a glass of apple juice when his father and mother drove up.

"Come and help carry," his mother called. She handed him the first grocery sack from the back seat. "Got your book for you," she said, following him into the house. She extracted it from one of the sacks she had carried in. "Here you are."

"Wow! It looks brand-new," said Gerald. "Thanks, Mom."

"Well, you'll have to thank Margaret. Her boy was never very interested in it. She was delighted to pass it on, she said."

Gerald took the book up to his room. Inside there was writing that said, "To Bobby from Aunt Helen, Christmas 1967," and underneath this some more writing that said, "A good book never dies, just gets passed on.

For Gerald from Margaret, 1985." Gerald smiled and turned to the big green map of Alaska. He studied it carefully. He located the red dot that was Fairbanks and the red arrow that pointed to the area designated as Deneki's home range. He rummaged around his desk until he found a red pen. Then he drew a lopsided egg around Fairbanks to show the range for his moose about the same

size as Deneki's. He thought about the moose and her calf browsing there, chewing the tender ends of miles and miles of willow, sleeping in the thickets with the sun warm on their backs, pulling at the grass that was getting thicker and greener every day.

Gerald smiled, turned the page, and settled down to read the book again.